THE SEVEN

TEACHINGS

The First People of America believe...
Long, long time ago, the Creator had a dream.
A dream of life.
From this dream Mother Earth was born,
a beautiful circle, full of life.
A sacred place where trees stretched towards the
sky, fish swam the rivers, animals roamed
the land and soon, we too came to live
among them.

We are all a part of the Creator's Circle of Life.
It was the Creator's wish that we live happy, peaceful lives and
remain connected to nature.
It is said that if you study nature you can see the face of the Creator.
To remind us of this way of life the Creator chose seven animals
to bring us Seven Sacred Teachings:

Eagle~ Love
Buffalo ~ Respect
Bear ~ Courage
Sabe ~ Honesty
Beaver ~ Wisdom
Wolf ~ Humility
Turtle ~ Truth

It is believed that if you live by
The Seven Teachings you will live a good and happy life.

EAGLE

From the sky Grandfather Eagle brings the
teaching of **Love** from the Creator.
Eagle teaches us:
Love the one who has given you the Seven Teachings – the Creator.
Love the Creator for the gift of life.
Love the Creator for giving you a beautiful home – Mother Earth.
Love will always overcome fear.
Love is most powerful.
Can you think of ways to show Love?

EAGLE ~ LOVE

5

BUFFALO

From the prairies came Grandfather Buffalo to bring
the teaching of **Respect** from the Creator.
Buffalo teaches us:
Respect is giving attention to your parents and elders.
Respect is about sharing with your family, friends and others.
Respect is about taking care of Mother Earth.
Respect is about taking care of you.
Can you think of ways to show Respect?

6

BUFFALO ~ RESPECT

BEAR

From the mountains came Grandfather Bear to bring
the teaching of **Courage** from the Creator.
Bear teaches us:
It takes Courage to be you.
Courage is being able to not agree when something is wrong.
Courage helps you to overcome difficult times or situations.
Courage helps you stand up for what is right.
It takes Courage to walk the Seven Teachings of life.
Can you think of ways to show Courage?

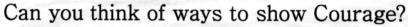

SABE

From deep in the forest came Grandfather Sabe to bring
the teaching of **Honesty** from the Creator.
Sabe teaches us:
Honesty means accepting who you are.
Honesty means telling the truth.
Honesty means not cheating, lying or stealing.
Honesty means keeping promises.
Can you think of ways to show Honesty?

SABE ~ HONESTY

BEAVER

From the rivers and creeks came Grandfather Beaver to bring
the teaching of **Wisdom** from the Creator.
Beaver teaches us:
Everyone has been given a special gift from the Creator.
Wisdom is realizing what your gift is and using it to help others.
The gift we are given will help us to build a world that is
full of love and peace.
Can you think of ways to show Wisdom?

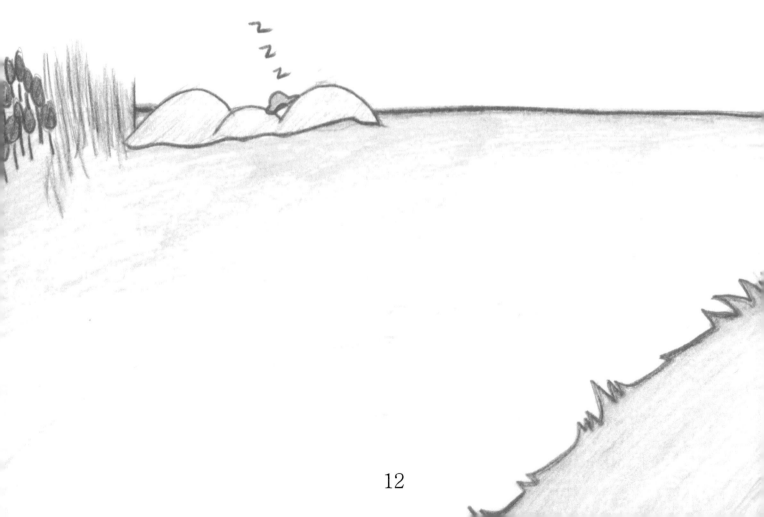

BEAVER ~ WISDOM

13

WOLF

From the wooded land came Grandfather Wolf to bring
the teaching of **Humility** from the Creator.
Wolf teaches us:
Being Humble means doing good things for other people.
Being Humble means that we are all equal whether we are
White, Black, Yellow or Red.
Can you think of ways to show Humility?

14

TURTLE

From the water and the land came Grandmother Turtle to bring the teaching of **Truth** from the Creator.

Grandmother Turtle has lived a very, very long time.

She was there when the Creator gave the Teachings to the other animals.

Grandmother **Turtle** teaches us:

Live by the Sacred Teachings – **Love, Respect, Courage, Honesty, Wisdom, Humility** and **Truth.**

Remember we are all a part of Mother Earth and the Circle of Life.

Can you think of ways to show Truth?

TURTLE ~ TRUTH

About the Author

David Courchene, Jr.,
Nii Gaani Aki Inini

Nii Gaani Aki Inini, a leader descended from a long line of leaders and chiefs of his people, the First Nations people of Turtle Island (America), learned the significance of the fire through a personal and spiritual quest for truth. Through the mentorship and the spiritual direction of the Elders, he was guided back to the ceremonies of his people. The Elders helped him realize that First Nations people, despite enduring generations of profound suffering, scarcity and hardship as a result of being displaced from their original connection to the land and a spiritual way of life, have survived because of the strength of the human spirit. The mentorship of the Elders provided Nii Gaani Aki Inini with inspiration, support, guidance and perspective on reaching a higher spiritual understanding, and a sense of the deep, sacred connection we have to the land.

David Courchene can be contacted at: turtlelodge@mts.net

Our mission is to efficiently provide the world's finest, most comprehensive book publishing service, enabling every author to experience success. To find out how to publish your book, your way, and have it available worldwide, visit us online at www.trafford.com

Any people depicted in stock imagery provided by Thinkstock are models,
and such images are being used for illustrative purposes only.
Certain stock imagery © Thinkstock.

Trafford rev. 06/17/2015

www.trafford.com
North America & international
toll-free: 1 888 232 4444 (USA & Canada)
fax: 812 355 4082

CPSIA information can be obtained at www.ICGtesting.com
Printed in the USA
LVIW01n2012230417
531915LV00002B/10